miss O™
& friends
by girls...for girls™

Write On!

The Miss O & Friends Collection of
ROCKIN' FICTION

Write On!

The Miss O & Friends Collection of
ROCKIN' FICTION

Illustrated by Hermine Brindak

Watson-Guptill Publications/New York

For all the girls out there who love to imagine, create, and write!

Senior Acquisitions Editor: Julie Mazur
Editor: Mikki Halpin
Designer: Edward Miller
Production Manager: Joseph Illidge

First published in 2006 by Watson-Guptill Publications,
a division of VNU Business Media, Inc.,
770 Broadway, New York, NY 10003
www.wgpub.com

Library of Congress Control Number: 2006923891

ISBN-10: 0-8230-2940-9
ISBN-13: 978-0-8230-2940-2

Printed in the United States of America

First printing, 2006

1 2 3 4 5 6 7 8 9 / 14 13 12 11 10 09 08 07 06

CONTENTS

juliette   isabella   miss O   harlie   justine

Meet the group!

Welcome to *Write On!*

When I, the real Juliette, was ten years old, I created the basis of Miss O and Friends. It started when I was on my way home from a family vacation. I was bored, so I borrowed some paper from my mom and started to draw "cool girls." I gave them to my mom, and like any mother would, she told me they were nice and put them in her purse. Little did she know that one day these drawings would turn into something much bigger.

Years later, with the help of my mom, my sister Olivia, and some friends, we started to create the Miss O girls. At first it was just something fun to do—we'd play around on the computer creating all sorts of ideas. It wasn't until we realized that girls really liked this stuff that the idea came to us to start a company. Now—thanks to girls like you—the Miss O and Friends website (www.missoandfriends.com) has become the most popular tween site ever!

When our website launched, we wanted to make sure it was interactive and that the community of girls using it felt like they were doing something great. This is how the writing contest got started. Girls would be able to use their creativity, imagination, and writing skills to share stories and experiences with the rest of the girls. And it wasn't just a great opportunity for self-expression—these girls had the chance to be published in an actual book!

Since then, thousands of stories and poems have been submitted and voted on by the Miss O community. About once a month, ten winners are picked, and many of their stories have ended up in this book. We wanted to share what we felt were the best of the best! Some are funny, some are sad. Some are based on real life, some on fantasy. The writers come from all over the United States, and there's even one from Thailand! But the one thing they *all* have in common is an ability to touch the reader.

Writing is a great way for girls (or anyone) to express themselves. When you're writing, you can't help but learn about who you are, what you stand for, and who you want to be. These are lessons that will help every girl as she grows up and faces problems and decisions in her life.

Our contest was created to inspire girls to start writing—and based on the amazing entries we received, it looks like we succeeded! Now people all over the country can see how talented these young writers are and how much they have to offer. So put on your sweatpants, get comfy in bed, and indulge yourself in a book of stories and poems by girls, for girls—just like you!

Juliette

At the Edge of the Universe
By Anya

At the edge of the universe
a poem hides
across the wide plains
of darkness.
At the end of a galaxy
a poem waits
waiting to be
uncovered.
When you find
that at the edge of the universe
a poem hides,
remember to
uncover her.
Always, always
look out for shy poems
like these
for many will
wait for millions, trillions of years
waiting
for a reader.

Anya is eleven years old and lives in Cohasset, Massachusetts.
Anya loves to write stories because she has so many creative
ideas she has to write them down to make room for more!

Do You Have the "Write" Stuff?

Want to submit your own story? Just log on to the Miss O and Friends website (www.missoandfriends.com), and click on "create." Then pick "submit a story." You can choose a topic and submit a story or poem up to 2,000 words.

Here are a few things to keep in mind when writing your story:

★ **Be creative.** The amazing thing about writing is that you have total freedom! You can tell a story from your own life, or you can make up characters, events, and places from your imagination or the world around you. Just be sure to pick an idea that excites you!

★ **Be original.** We want to hear *your* thoughts and feelings, not someone else's! Copying a story from the Internet or elsewhere will automatically disqualify your story from the contest.

★ **Think it through.** Take a few minutes to think about your story before you start writing. What is the main idea? Does it have a beginning, middle, and end? Try to summarize your story in only one sentence. Can you? If not, think about it some more until you can!

★ **Keep it real.** The best stories are those that show the personality of the writer. Don't worry too much about using long words or perfect sentences. Put your personality into your story and it will be much more fun for others to read!

★ **Give yourself a break.** Sometimes if you're feeling stuck, it helps to take a break from your story. Talk to a friend, go for a walk, have something to eat—anything to give your brain a rest! Later, when you're ready, come back and read your story again. You may find that you want to change some things, or you may love it just the way it is!

★ **Check it out.** Always check your spelling. This is an easy thing to do, but it makes a big difference.

★ **Play the name game.** Don't forget to give your story or poem a great title!

Good luck!

FRIENDSHIP

"A best friend is like a four-leaf clover—
hard to find and lucky to have."
—*Anonymous*

Practical Joker or Practical Jokee?

By Ashley

I couldn't believe it. School was finally over! It was the end of my eighth-grade year, and to celebrate I was having a few friends sleep over. The last time I had a sleepover, I'd played a bunch of practical jokes on my friends that they didn't really like, so it took a lot of coaxing to get them to agree to come . . . and a little lying.

I was on the phone with my best friend, Stacey. "Stacey, you gotta come. Pleeaase?"

"Not after all the stupid jokes you pulled last time," she said. At the last sleepover, I put purple (the color she hates most) hair dye in her shampoo. Hey, she's my best friend; I had to save my best joke for her.

"Stacey, I promise that I won't do any of that stuff this time," I said. I was totally lying, but she fell for it.

"Promise?" she asked doubtfully.

"Cross my heart," I reassured her. "See ya Saturday night," I said as I hung up the phone and crossed her name off my list.

She was the last one, so I had Stacey, Brittney, Whittney, Kiera, and Nikki down to attend my party Saturday night. Now all I had to do was come up with some fabulous practical jokes to pull. I sat down and put my brilliant mind to work.

* * *

The night of the party, I was in the kitchen gathering snacks when the doorbell rang. Great! My first guest was here. I rushed toward the door, but my annoying younger brother Bryan got there first. He was just about to open it when I grabbed his arm. "Bryan, MOVE!" I ordered.

"You're not the boss of me," he retorted.

"Fine, but I know who is. Mom!" I started to yell.

"Okay, okay, bossy," he cut me off as he stormed out of the room. I knew that would work—Mom had made him promise to stay in his room, out of our way.

I opened the door to reveal Stacey on the other side. Of course she was the first to arrive. Everyone else arrived pretty soon after that.

When everyone was there, we stampeded up to my room with snacks and DVDs. At about 10:30, we started rolling out our sleeping bags and changing into our pajamas. It was time for the show to begin!

I was just about to launch my first practical joke when the lights went out! The house was in complete and total darkness. My party guests started to yell at me.

"Ashley, you promised," Stacey whined.

"Yeah," Brittney chimed in.

"You said you wouldn't pull any of these stupid jokes. Now turn the lights back on!" yelled Nikki. She was still a little afraid of the dark. Too many horror movies, I guess.

"You guys, it's not me. You gotta believe me," I pleaded with them. "Let's go find my mom and dad. They'll know what to do," I said. To myself, I wondered if there was anything we *could* do, but I didn't dare say it. I, too, was still just a little bit afraid of the dark. Hey, like I said, too many horror movies.

We each grabbed someone else's hand and formed a human chain. We started slowly down the staircase with me leading the way, Stacey backing me up, Kiera behind her, and Nikki bringing up the rear.

"Nikki, what are you doing?" Kiera asked as she felt Nikki let go of her hand. She looked behind her where Nikki was supposed to be, but Nikki wasn't there. "Oh my gosh! Nikki's gone!" Kiera yelled. That's when I really got scared.

One by one, the girls disappeared, until I was left with no hand to hold. I panicked. "Mom, Dad!" I called, and (I was desperate) "Bryan!" That's when I saw a human shadow pass the window. I turned and started to run back upstairs. I was halfway to my room when the lights came back on.

"GOTCHA!" everyone yelled as a camera flashed in my face.

That picture of my horrified face now hangs on our living room wall. Every time I see it, I am reminded of the night I got a taste of my own medicine. The sleepover horror really taught me a lesson. No more practical jokes for me . . . EVER!

Ashley is fifteen and lives in Thomasville, Georgia. She likes to write because she was read to as a child and she grew to love books.

Best Friends
By Emily

Annie always knew when Nikki was mad. They were, after all, best friends forever. Nikki's bright green eyes would darken and narrow, then she would flip her long brown hair and place a hand on her hip, slightly leaning forward, as if to take the problem head on. She was doing all of those things right now. Annie knew something was up.

"Aw, come on, Nikki, give me a smile, please? What's wrong?" asked Annie, leaning against the school wall.

Nikki stuck her nose in the air. "Nothing that you need to know, Anna."

Annie's jaw dropped. "Anna? Come on, you know that I hate my full name."

Nikki sighed. She grabbed her books and said, "Maybe we don't know

so much about each other." Nikki spun on her heel, making her sneakers squeak and walked away with confidence. Nikki was always so emotional.

Annie sighed. Life was hard enough. They were in sixth grade now, the youngest kids at Brook Middle School. The school was bigger, badder, and scarier than their elementary school. Why did Nikki have to make it even worse? Annie raced to class as the bell rang.

After school Annie waited outside for Nikki. She finally saw Nikki slink out. Nikki seemed to slouch as she slugged along. "Come on, Nikki! Let's go! Why were you late? Everyone else left. Do you want to talk? I'm worried about you," Annie said, wondering how Nikki would react. Annie had gotten a little scared of Nikki lately. She was intimidating.

Nikki narrowed her darkening green eyes. "Shut up, Annie. Stay out of my life. Nothing is wrong. The only thing wrong is talking to you! As of now, we are no longer best friends! I hate you!" Nikki shouted. She ran away, her backpack bouncing angrily on her shoulders.

Annie was hurt. It was weird, but Nikki was the only reason Annie had been happy. Nikki completed her. Now she had no one to talk to the way she always had with Nikki. Annie was alone.

The next day, Annie's day went by more slowly than ever, but she didn't care. Her life didn't matter. Nikki hated her. School hated her. Life hated her.

Annie's friend Sarah popped up next to Annie as she was eating lunch. "Hey, do you know what's with Nikki?" Sarah asked Annie, a concerned look on her face.

Annie shrugged and said, "Nikki hates me."

Their friend Mimi sat down. "I know why," she offered. "Nikki is under stress. I saw her yesterday. She has piles of homework and her parents have high expectations."

Annie nodded slowly. "Yeah. Her parents want her to be perfect," she agreed.

"Oh, yeah, and she's afraid to lose you, Annie," Mimi added.

"Why?" Annie wondered.

Mimi sighed and told her, "Because you guys have been friends forever. And Nikki heard that you don't like her from someone. So she's trying to dump you before you can dump her. She doesn't want to get hurt. Nikki relies on you, Annie." This was new. Annie had never said she hated Nikki. Annie realized what she had to do. She had to apologize to Nikki and straighten things out.

Annie again waited for Nikki after school. She saw Nikki walk out. "Nikki!" Annie called out, "Can we talk?" Nikki nodded. They walked over to a tree and sat in its shade. "So, Nikki. I heard that you thought I hated you. Gosh, Nikki, I would never say that! We're best friends. I love you like a sister!" Annie said, gulping. Would Nikki understand?

Nikki hugged Annie tight. "Oh, Annie, I was afraid to lose you! I love you like a *twin* sister! I'm sorry. My feelings got out of control. I wish I'd never said that we weren't best friends. Best friends now?" Nikki asked.

Annie grinned. "Of course. Best friends," she said, hugging Nikki again.

They were best friends again, just like always. Annie wasn't alone anymore. Nikki was there for her. They were, and always would be, best friends forever.

Emily is thirteen and lives in Essex Junction, Vermont. Emily loves to write because she can express herself freely. Stories appeal to her because she can make something up and imagine herself in it.

I Am
By Kelsey

I am
A spring rain when you need calm
A summer sky when you need comfort
A sun when you're blue
A delicate flower when you need peace
A blank diary when you want to pour out your soul
A shoulder when you need to cry
A friend when you need a hug
A scrapbook when you recall memories
A puppy when you need love and warmth
A song when you need music
A friend whenever.

Kelsey is twelve and lives in Camden-Wyoming, Delaware. She likes to use her creativity to develop characters, stories, and settings that transport her to different places and times. She enjoys writing realistic fiction most but is also happy to write poetry.

Any Time You Need a Friend
By Marissa

Mandy sat quietly on her doorstep, sobbing about everything that had been happening to her. Her parents had recently divorced, and she had to move from Los Angeles to New York City with her mom. Mandy was a little girl in a big city. She had left all her friends behind in California, so she didn't have any friends to play with any more. She only had friends to email, send letters to, and talk to on the phone. Mandy's dad had moved to Nashville, Tennessee, with her older sister and her dog, Pepper.

The day after she moved to New York, Mandy went to school, as usual, but it was a different school, with different people, and nobody to talk to. During lunch, nobody even sat next to her. People laughed at her and called her names, like "Newbie" and "Loser." Mandy ran home crying. She ran up the steps into her room and slammed the door. Just then, she heard a knock on the door. "Come in," she murmured, trying to catch her breath under her tears.

"Are you okay, honey?" asked her mom. "You seemed very upset when you came into the house."

"I had a horrible day at school today. Everyone laughed me, and it didn't make me feel very good. I didn't know *anyone*, to top it all off! I miss home! I miss my friends! I miss California!"

"Well, honey," her mom explained, "You need to try and make friends. Just be yourself, the kind little child I know, and somebody's bound to make friends with you. Maybe you should go on a walk to calm yourself down."

"Okay," Mandy replied, "I'll be back before sunset. Bye, I love you!" Mandy ran out the door, still half wet from crying, not knowing that something she'd been waiting for was about to happen.

Mandy walked down the block and looked back at her house to make sure she knew which house she lived in, because it was fairly new to her. As she looked back, she felt a thump from behind and came crashing down on the sidewalk. She looked up and saw a girl she remembered from her school cafeteria on the ground as well.

"I'm so sorry! I'll help you up and move out of your way. Please don't be mad at me!" said the girl, seeming very frightened.

"Mad?" Mandy asked. "I'm not mad at you. If anything, it was my fault because I was looking back when I really shouldn't have been. Don't be frightened of me. I would never hurt anybody. You go to PS19, right?"

"Yes," answered the girl. "How did you know that?"

"Because that's my new school," Mandy said. "I know we don't really know each other, but would you like to take a walk with me?"

"Me? *You* want *me* to take a walk with you?" the girl asked. "I'd love to! Oh, and by the way, my name's Brianna. Oh, sorry I'm talking too fast again! Nobody *ever* talks to me! What's your name?"

"Mandy," she replied as they started walking slowly. "I just moved here from Los Angeles, two days ago. My dad, older sister, and dog live in Nashville, and my mom lives with me here. My parents just went through a divorce a month ago, so I'm only starting to get used to it. I've been longing for new friends from New York because I left all my friends behind."

"Oh. I'm sorry," said Brianna thoughtfully. "I didn't know, really. So, do you want *me* to be your friend? I'd love to be your friend, not only because I don't have any friends, but because you don't have any friends, either. We'd be perfect together! Two friendless girls coming together and being friends!"

"Thank you so much, Brianna," Mandy said cheerfully. "Would you like to come over and meet my mother?"

"Yes," answered Brianna. "Definitely!"

"Mom! I'm home," yelled Mandy as she ran through the door.

"Feel any better, honey?" asked her mom.

"Yes, much better. I brought someone home with me. Mom, meet Brianna, my new friend," replied Mandy.

"Hello, Brianna. It's very nice to meet you. I'm Mandy's mom, as you probably already know," her mother introduced herself.

For the next few hours, Brianna stayed over Mandy's house. They played and talked together. Brianna would never know just how grateful Mandy was that she had a friend. And it wasn't just for all of the fun stuff, but to be there for her at times when she really needed a friend.

"Any time you need a friend, I'll be there for you," said Brianna.

Mandy replied, "Me too!"

Marissa is eleven and lives in Commack, New York. She enjoys writing because she loves to be creative, and writing is a way to express her creativity.

A Different Path

By Nesima

It was near the end of elementary school and Nicole, Keisha, and Maggie couldn't wait for middle school. They thought of the fun of going to different classes, meeting new people, learning new things, and trying out for different clubs or sports. Middle school seemed to be the answer to all their problems.

"I wonder if we'll like Dakota Middle School?" wondered Nicole as they sat in her bedroom one afternoon.

"I think so! It's going to be awesome!" said Keisha, who was the most optimistic of the friends.

"I'm kind of worried that the classes will get too hard or the teachers will be really mean. What if we get lost on the first day? That would be horrible!" Maggie worried aloud, biting her thumbnail. They sighed.

"At least we'll all be together. It won't be so bad," said Nicole. Keisha and Maggie nodded in agreement. Just then the door opened and Nicole's mom came in.

"Keisha, your mother just called and said you need to get home. And it is getting late so your parents will be expecting you, too, Maggie," she announced. The girls hugged goodbye, and Nicole watched them leave.

"Nicole, I want to talk to you about something," her mom began. "We heard about this school from a friend of mine at work. It's a very good school, their curriculum is advanced, and their test scores are higher than those of the public schools here." Nicole looked up from her book with a questioning face.

"So?"

"We're thinking of enrolling you there for sixth grade. They have smaller classes, so you'll get more attention, and they have lots of good art and music programs, even a writing club—you'll like that."

Nicole knew where this was going. She tried to remain calm. "That's nice, but I'm going to Dakota anyway," she answered, going back to her book.

Her mom pulled out a brochure. "Here. Look at this and think about it. It will be good—I know you'll like it. We want the very best for you, and my friend's kids love it there." Nicole's mom walked out of the room. Nicole picked up the brochure and stared at the smiling kids holding pencils and reaching for the sky with a teacher next to them.

No. No, she can't do this to me. I'm not leaving my friends to go to some stupid genius school. I'm not going, thought Nicole. Maggie and Keisha would hate her forever if she went to a different middle school. What was it called, anyway? She read the front: Great Minds Academy. Nice name . . . not. She stood up and walked to the kitchen, where she knew her mom would be preparing dinner.

"Mom, why do you want me to go there? Why can't I go to Dakota?" she asked. "Everyone else is going there, and it's only three blocks from our house. It makes more sense to go there. You already said that I would go there too."

Nicole's mom set down the spatula. "We want the best education for you—these are the years that count. Dakota is doing reasonably well, but Great Minds is doing even better. Don't you want to enter high school with a good background?"

Her mom was right, but Nicole still didn't want to give in.

"It's not fair—you never told me about this. I already told my friends

I'm going to Dakota, and I want to stay with them!" Her voice rose. Nicole's mom turned around.

"Nicole, you don't go to school for your friends. You go to learn. You can still see Keisha and Maggie on the weekends and after school—we're not preventing you from seeing them. Daddy agrees with me. Enrolling you there will be good, and then your sister will go there with you."

"But Emmaleigh is going into third grade—that's not middle school," Nicole said, crossing her arms.

"This academy is kindergarten through eighth grade. That's another reason we like it—we will have both of you at one school. We have you on a waiting list and we'll hear from them soon," her mom said firmly.

Nicole frowned and stomped to her room. They didn't even ask my opinion—they've already decided, she thought. She was just pretending to ask me what I think. Nicole slumped on her bed, picked up her telephone, and dialed.

"Hello?"

"Hello, is Kiesha there?"

"This is Keisha."

"Hey, this Nicole."

"Oh, hey. Why do you sound so glum?"

"I'm not going to Dakota," Nicole started to say, waiting for Keisha to scream.

"What? Say that again? Not going to Dakota? But . . . ," Keisha said slowly.

"My wonderful parents decided to go behind my back and put me in some academy school that's smarter than Dakota," Nicole grumbled.

"No way! Is it that Great Minds one? Yeah, my mom wanted to put me there but I refused, so I'm still going to Dakota. Why don't you tell her you don't want to?" Keisha asked.

"I tried, but it's no use. Both my parents think it's a good idea."

"Awww. Well I'll call Maggie and we'll think of something, don't worry. Call you later, okay? Love ya!" Keisha exclaimed.

"All right, see ya," Nicole said and hung up. She traced an outline on her bed sheets with her finger and thought. All of their lives they'd thought about going to Dakota—the big school with the big kids who did the coolest things. And now it would just be Maggie and Keisha. Oh no! Nicole panicked. What if they get new friends and forget me? She hadn't even thought of that part. What if they change and think I'm weird? She didn't want to be labeled as one of those smarty kids who goes to an academy. Why did her parents have to be so cruel?

The next day Nicole's parents took her to view her new school. It was very preppy and looked almost like a small resort. There were nicely painted walls, clean and neat classrooms, new equipment, and a large lunchroom. The principal gave the tour and told them about all the awards the school had gotten in art contests, science fairs, and reading competitions. They even had a small school farm with real animals.

It all sounded nice, but Nicole was determined to hate it. Her sister, on the other hand, was excited and asked questions like whether they got to play with the animals and if they served cookies at lunch. The one thing that interested Nicole was the library. It was so polished, with dark oak bookshelves, comfortable lounge chairs, tables, and computers. It even smelled good. Her parents looked at her to see what she thought.

"Um, it's okay, I guess," she muttered.

"I understand how you feel about leaving your friends," Nicole's mom told her. "It will be hard. But we're not moving—you can still see them. We just want you to have the best, you know that. We thought of everything before enrolling you here. In three years you'll join your friends in high school, and you can look forward to that, honey." Nicole shrugged and nodded.

Her mom kept going. "We all have to go down different paths, sweetie, and sometimes they're not the ones we want. But you'll meet up with Maggie and Keisha again. They're are great friends and you will always be together, no matter what."

Nicole smiled at that. Her mom was right. Keisha would do whatever it would take to see her all the time, and Maggie would always want Nicole to be happy and to be her friend. Maybe it wouldn't be so bad after all.

Nesima is fifteen and lives in Chandler, Arizona. She loves to write stories because it's a way to always hold on to your youth and have fun by yourself.

FAMILY

"Families are like fudge—
mostly sweet with a few nuts."
—*Anonymous*

The Most Totally Weird Family EVER (Seriously!)
By Emily

Yeah, yeah, everyone thinks their family is *sooooo* terrible. But my family is the worst. Do they show my friends embarrassing butt-naked baby photos? No. Do they wear the fashion "don'ts" of the century? Nope. Have they told a guy I like to tuck in his shirttail? Goose eggs. THEY'VE DONE IT ALL TEN TIMES WORSE!!!!!! We're talking *five* naked-baby-butt pictures, the fashion don'ts of the century *before last,* and telling the guy I like that his new (totally rad) shoes were *ugly*!! Yes, they are THE WORST, MOST TOTALLY IGNORANT FAMILY A GIRL COULD EVER HAVE!!! And this is the story of how they officially ruined my life. Get ready for a rollercoaster ride, ladies and gentlemen.

It was Family Fun Day. The most dreaded day of a sixth-grade girl's life. Principal Wigby gave the opening announcement. "Welcome parents, students, teachers, to Dooleywinker Middle School's first annual Family Fun Day!" (The annoying parents, including mine, started to clap. UGH!) "We'd love for you to participate in the slime pool, the relay race, and the balloon slides—all just a dollar each! And don't forget the popcorn, cotton candy, and soda over at the concession stand! Let the day begin!"

The kids with normal parents all skipped away to enjoy the day. I groaned. Mom grabbed my hand and pulled me away toward the torture—I mean the *slime*—pool.

"A buck each, please," said the lunch lady, who was running the slime pool. Mom handed her three dollars, and we prepared to hurl balls at a red circle, trying to knock Principal Wigby into the pool of slime. This, at least, could be enjoyable.

"Aha! Whizzer idea coming on, sweetums!" said Dad. I hate Dad's whizzer ideas. "You can sit beside Mr. Wigby and we'll take a picture!" Mr. Wigby, hearing us, tried to conceal an evil smirk.

"You brought a *camera*?!" I asked. "I don't want to have to relive this day *ever*!"

"Of course we did! Now get your patoot up there so we can take your pic!"

Pic? UGH!!! I climbed into the Pit of Doom and sat awkwardly next to the principal. Ugh-er. Dad aimed the camera while Mom chucked balls at the Red Circle of Death (or Red Circle of Pain—whichever works for you).

POW!! The fatal battle of ball vs. red circle ended . . . and the ball won. Principal Wigby and I fell into the green glob puddle just as the school hottie—a.k.a. Robbie the Hottie—walked by. Covered in goo, I could hear the principal screaming (or was that me?), Dad's camera clicking, and Robbie and everyone else laughing. This was not good.

I climbed out of the pool and rushed into the girl's room, splotches of green trailing behind me. I tried to hide my sniffles when my mom came into the bathroom (thankfully not followed by anyone).

"You okay?" she asked.

"Go away."

"Sweetheart, I know we're a little wacky sometimes, but it's because we love you. We want to have fun with you. When your father and I were young, we were always ignored or busy taking care of our siblings. Please forgive us. We'll try to be cool."

Aww! Who could say no to that?! "I love you, Mom," I said, coming out of the stall. We hugged. And, well, for once I'll admit I was wrong. My family really isn't quite as bad as I make them out to be. I love them . . . sometimes. (Just kidding!!!)

Emily is twelve and lives in Little Rock, Arkansas. She loves to write stories because she believes that writing is a way to live through someone else by using your imagination.

A Different Kind of Hero
By Sarah

Some people think a hero is somebody who can fly and
    has laser vision,
Who can pick up a car or has big muscles and a cape.
But that isn't what a real hero is.
No, my hero is a different kind of hero.
This hero can't fly or read people's minds.
She can't turn into an animal or go through walls.
Nor can she sit on the moon or touch the sky, or even walk
    on a cloud.
But you know what she can do?
She can dry my tears and soothe my fears.
When I have no hope left in my heart, she pulls some out of
    a magic hat and gives it to me as a present.
She helps me reach my goals and fulfill my dreams.
She's always there for me . . . from a broken heart to a
    broken doll.
She gives me a shoulder to lean on all day, every day.
    She cries with me.
    She laughs with me.
    She sings with me.
    She talks with me.

My hero doesn't give up on me.

If I need to talk, or I need a helping hand, or if I just want to
go to the beach and feel the sand . . . it doesn't matter to
her, she'll be there.

She gives me courage and faith in everything I do.

This hero can't be destroyed or beaten, and she's never failed
with helping me or anyone else.

Even if she's not like Batman or Wonder Woman, she's still a
hero.

My hero.

My mom.

Sarah is twelve and lives in Moreno Valley, California. She
likes writing stories and poetry as an outlet for her emotions.
Sometimes she can make a whole story from just a name.

Speak Your Mind
By Jamie

Dribble, block, kick, and score! "Yes! I did it!" I yelled.

"Good job, Jane, you should try out for the team!" Ms. Deriz, the soccer coach, called across the field.

"Oh my gosh, she was watching me!" I thought. "I will think on it!" I called back to the coach.

Going home in high spirits, I got off the bus and ran inside. My dad greeted me as I entered the living room. "Hey honey! How was school?" he asked me.

"Great!" I told him with a grin.

"This day will get even better. Go look upstairs on your bed!" he ordered.

"Okay," I said. "But first, here's this paper I got at school. I can sign up to do soccer, volleyball, football, or basketball," I told him, handing over the paper and racing upstairs.

There on my bed was a new DVD! It was for my new DVD player. I looked at the title: "Basketball Players of the Season." Ugh, more basketball! My dad thinks I like basketball. It was his dream for me to join the school team. I couldn't tell him that I hated basketball and loved soccer. It would break his determined heart. I put the DVD on and pressed play. "I might as well watch it to get some tips," I thought, full of the blues.

The next day, as I was going outside to catch the bus, my dad gave me back the paper. He had signed me up for basketball. I could see how happy he was, but to me it was heartbreaking. At school, all my friends asked if I had joined the soccer team. I told them I was doing basketball instead. My best friend Mia could tell there was more to it.

"Is it your dad again?" she asked.

"You better believe it." I said glumly.

"You need to tell him you *don't* want to take basketball and you *do* want to take soccer," she said. "He will understand. If not, you can blame it on me, okay?"

I put my head in my hands. "I can't do it," I murmured.

"Yes you can," she urged me. "Nothing will happen if you won't tell him. You will keep on playing basketball, and he will keep on thinking you love it. You know he only signed you up for basketball because he loves you and thinks it's what you want." She was right and I knew it. I hate it when she is right, because she is always right. It is not fair. I want to always be right. Ugh!!!

When I got home from school that day, I entered my house with determination. I was going to tell him. "Dad," I started. Then I looked up at him. I could not do it. His kind, loving eyes were too much.

"What is it?" he asked.

"Nothing, never mind." I said.

"I just couldn't do it." I told Mia the next day.

"That's okay. You will do it when you are ready. I know you have it in you, Jane." Mia said.

Later that day, I had my first basketball practice. It went well, except that all the other girls were a foot or two taller than I was. That night I sat on my bed watching a video from when I was six. My dad had made it, and it starred my mom and me. In the beginning my mom asks me, "Jane, do you want to be a movie star?" and I reply, "No! I want to be a writer and write about puppies." Then in the movie I become a writer who writes about puppies. Later on, I am in a restaurant, and my mother is the server. She asks me, "Would you like fries and a burger, Madam?" "No! I want fries and chicken," I tell her. And then I get fries and chicken.

I lay in bed, thinking about the movie and how my mother did just what I asked of her. Would my dad do that with soccer? I didn't think he would. I drifted to sleep with the burden of not knowing.

The next week, my basketball team had our first game. Of course, my dad was going to be there, cheering me on to do what I was dreading. When I arrived at the basketball court, I felt a chill go up my spine. I was *not* ready. I did not want to be there.

I nervously approached my extremely tall team. I looked up into the crowd. There he was, my dad, looking so proud of me. He gave me a thumbs-up. I gulped and waved. I was also nervous because I really was not the best player on my team. I had not scored a single point, ever. I did not expect this game to be any different.

I was right. By the middle of the game I had failed to score, and my team was behind by one point. Then, all of a sudden, things changed. A player on the other team tried to pass the ball, but instead it came right to me! I caught the ball and began dribbling up the court. I had confidence—I knew I could do it! A large opposing player tried to block me, but I dodged her. I had gotten this far; she was not going to get in my way! I jumped as high as I could, took my shot, and lobbed the ball into the hoop.

The crowed went wild. I ran up the stands to my dad. He looked so proud! "Great job, sweetie!" he yelled, scooping me into a hug.

"Dad, I have to talk to you," I said. "I never really liked basketball. I only played on this team to make you happy. I really wanted to play soccer."

My dad looked at me, surprised. "You should have told me! You can start soccer right away! I will support whatever you want to do!" he said. But I wasn't done telling him what I had to say.

"That's what I thought before," I told him, "but now I know that my dream has been basketball all along. I just had to figure it out!"

Jamie is twelve and lives in Tampa, Florida. She says that writing is her passion because you get to create emotions and feelings and dream up a person's life.

GROWING PAINS

"In a world where you can be
anything, be yourself."
—*Anonymous*

The Quest for Normal
By Maddie

"What is normal?" my religion teacher asked yesterday at the start of class.

One of the boys replied, "Nothing! Everybody's a monkey!"

Several snickers ran through the classroom, but Mr. Cherbin took no notice. "Exactly correct, Frankie!" he boomed. "There is no such thing as normal. In fact, everyone in here is differently unique . . . ." As usual, he droned on and on, but his question stuck to my mind like duct tape.

"What is normal?" The more I thought about it, the more convinced I was that there was such a thing as normal—and that I should go on a quest to become it.

When I talked with my best friend Melissa that night, we decided to end our extraordinary lives and become "normal." Taking her advice, I regretfully handed all my glittery shirts to my younger sister, who squealed at the sight of them. I then took all my astronaut posters down and tacked up celebrities in their place. The printer ran out of ink as I tried to find regular hairstyles. (That was my bad.) The hairstyles made me wince as I tried them. They looked so . . . blah. I grimly reminded myself that this was how regular girls wore their hair, and it was all worth it to be absolutely normal. I went to bed that night feeling like a huge part of me was missing.

The next morning, I woke up from a horrible dream about a little elf wearing orange and purple striped socks. The elf was squeaking, "Kayla, you shalt not be normal!"

"Oh yeah?" I challenged. "Who are you, God?"

The elf merely bowed and replied humbly, "Hey kid, you never know." It disappeared, and I sighed with relief. But the next moment, hundreds of elves wearing hideous outfits popped out from nowhere, chanting, "Not normal! Not normal!" I woke up sweating. (Though I don't know why. I mean, who's scared of elves anyway?) Even though I had a ton of other things to worry about, I kept thinking of those elves. Were they trying to say something to me? Oh, well. It was time for the new, normal me.

When I entered the school doors with Melissa, I could have sworn I heard people's eyes bugging out of their heads. There was (strangely) a dead silence the whole time we walked to our lockers. "What's up with them?" I asked Melissa uncomfortably.

"Oh, they're just in pure shock. No big," she answered.

Still, I couldn't help but wish everybody would just mind their own business. So what if we had plain pigtails, plain clothes, plain personalities? We were just exactly regular. Unfortunately, not everyone saw it that way. Take the rest of our group, for example.

"What do you think you're doing?" they demanded of us at lunch. I shrugged my shoulders and continued eating my taco. "Well we don't like it. You're out." They snapped their fingers, then flashed the palms of their hands at Melissa and me. They walked away without looking back.

Another group who noticed the change was our teachers. Yesterday, Melissa and I were the girls who always had our hands raised before the teacher was done talking. Today, we were slumped in our chairs like half of the class.

"Kayla? Melissa? Don't you have anything to contribute?" they asked.

"No," we replied, very politely. Then they'd continue their lesson, but my brain was longing to scream out corrections. I was fully convinced that today was the hardest day of my life.

At long last, the school day was finally over. I boarded the bus to face the remaining fifteen minutes of being in public until I got home. And that's where the real trouble started. Some of the boys in my grade began to poke fun at me.

"Oooh. What's the matter, Kayla? Scawed of widdew schoow?"

I replied with my head held up high, "No."

They continued. "Widdew Kaywa is afwaid of schoow. She can't even answer the qwestions when hew teachew tews hew to."

"Not true," I said, defending myself.

Frankie sat himself down in the seat in front of me at the next stop. "What's wrong with you, Kayla?" he asked gently.

"Nothing," I stiffly replied.

He glanced back at the driver to make sure he wasn't looking, then slid into my seat. "Something's wrong, I can tell."

"How can you tell?" I eyed him suspiciously.

He started listing points off his fingers. "First, you were almost completely silent all day. Second, you're dressed completely plain. Third, well, I can sense when something's going on." He grinned at me. "Are those good enough reasons? Will you tell me?" He gave me these totally sarcastic puppy-dog eyes. I had to tell him. If I didn't tell anyone soon, I was going to explode like a shaken-up soda can.

I told Frankie absolutely everything. He listened intently the whole time. Finally, he took a long, slow breath and said, "So, Mr. Cherbin totally freaked you out."

"Well, yeah, I guess so."

He peered right into my face and asked me, "Do you want to be completely normal?"

Startled, I couldn't get the right words out. "Well, yes, but no, I mean yes, no, I guess not."

"So don't be. Be the Kayla I know. Be the Kayla everyone around this old place is familiar with, and leave the normalness to me," he told me.

The bus pulled up to my stop, and Frankie stood up so I could get out. As I exited the bus, he called out, "Don't forget now, ya hear?" I looked back, smiled, and nodded at him. I stepped off the bus feeling completely Kayla-ish.

And that was completely normal.

Maddie is eleven and lives in Savage, Minnesota. She says that writing is her way of connecting with the rest of the world. She responds to things happening to her and to things about life.

Peer Pressure
By Rita

"Wow."

That was Justine, my BFF. We were standing outside Clague Middle School, gazing up at the tangle of students pushing their way in. Justine shook her head and tsked. "This isn't a school, it's a educational jungle."

I nodded in agreement and sighed, "It's survival of the fittest." I squared my shoulders and started marching toward the wild crowd of students.

"Juliette, you've gone AWOL. I say we wait until these monkeys are out of the way and then make our move," Justine declared.

"I'm not going to be late for class again," I called over my shoulder. Justine rolled her eyes and followed me. All of a sudden, the mass in front of the doors started parting. Right away, I knew what had caused it. Carla Henderson, Queen Bee and Detention Ruler of Clague, was pushing her way into the school. Her blond head was held high, her perfectly manicured hands on her hips.

Justine started to move out of her way, but I stayed where I was. "You're not going to obey her are you?" I demanded. My friend just shrugged.

Carla walked right up to me. "Move it or lose it, DORK!" She barely glanced at me while talking. I was glued to the ground, furious at her. Dork? At least I pass class!

"Not going to happen," I said quietly. Carla's head snapped down and she glared at me. Justine twitched nervously.

"What did you just say to me?"

"I said, 'Not going to happen,'" I said more loudly.

"You are going to pay," Carla snarled, shouldering her way past me.

"Great. I have a slice of future social toast for a best friend," Justine grinned jokingly.

Things went on pretty normally until English class. Since English is my best subject, I have no trouble getting straight As. "Great job, Juliette!" my teacher smiled at me. "Another A plus!" I smiled back and bent back over my persuasive creative writing essay. When she moved on, I heard a snicker from behind. Carla had chosen to sit in the seat directly behind me.

"Well, if it isn't Miss Know-it-All," she whispered snidely. "You're such a geek. You're a teacher's pet and a suck-up!"

"Oh, yeah. That's right! You have an F minus, don't you, Carla?" I kept my head and retorted. I returned to writing.

Half an hour had passed when the teacher finally announced, "Put your pencils away, class. Time to share your essays. Would you like to go first, Juliette?" I nodded in reply. I had spent a lot of time rewriting my essay to convey my new message. It had become a masterpiece and I was really proud of it.

I got up to the front of the room and smirked at Carla, who glared back. "My essay is actually more of an article," I began. "I tried to convince the target audience that being smart doesn't necessarily mean you are a geek." I glanced at Carla and almost grinned at the angry look on her face.

I took a deep breath and started to read. "Ever been called a geek for being a straight-A student? It hurts and makes you confused, right? But next time you feel like slacking off your work to get a lower grade, keep in mind that you can be both smart and cool. Getting good grades means getting a good education, which leads to moolah-making jobs. The kids who have bad grades will have a harder time getting jobs later in life. These same kids know what they're in for, so they aren't very smart if they continue to act that way. Keep a cool, confident air if you're smart, because now you know—you're cool!"

There was a moment of complete silence. Then, slowly, applause started to grow louder and louder. Soon, people were cheering and whistling. Carla looked furious and embarrassed. The teacher had an uncertain look on her face. "Well, that essay was certainly enlightening," she said finally. "But Juliette is right. Being smart is a 'cool' quality. It certainly pays to keep up good grades."

I caught Justine's eye and winked. She smiled back and mouthed, "Score one for the geeks!"

Rita is twelve and lives in Bangkok, Thailand. She enjoys using words to create new ideas and new worlds. In her eyes, writing is the greatest form of expression.

Untitled

By Afi

Thinking about when I grow up
About when I die
About extinction
About butterflies
About best friends
About me
Thinking . . .
Thinking . . .
Thinking about life.

Afi is twelve and lives in Woodstock, Georgia. She likes to write stories using different characters to express how she feels.

Looking Down the Barrel of a Rifle Named Eve
By Abby

People never really stop to think about the reason that one girl jumps into their world. I mean, most people just assume it's because they wore a plain cotton belt, or a skirt past their knees, or braids instead of a bun. But they're wrong. I should know.

I can't say why exactly Eve came into my life the way she did. Maybe it was my mop of short curly hair that never seems brushed, or the fact that I have a pet mouse. But most likely of all it was the fact that I am shy.

Crowd Girls, or CGs, look for your emotional reactions to things, your personality, and your sore spots. If you have a tendency to get upset about things like zoos, for example, they will find out and research the tortures animals experience in cages in order to torment you. Because I was a new kid at Raynetire Junior High, the CGs' instincts were immediately focused on me. Everyone could tell that I was shy, and no one was friendly. I was isolated and vulnerable. Crowd Girls thrive off that.

One girl, Cara, was chosen to "befriend" me. Within a week, she managed to wrangle my secrets out—I worried about my hair, I had a mouse, and I was incredibly shy. The next Monday, when I came by her house to meet her before school, she wasn't there, and I was almost late because of standing there waiting by her gate. When I heard the bell, I broke into a run and rounded the corner of the schoolyard with five minutes to spare.

I should've been late.

Rotten apples appeared from nowhere, pelting my back. I ducked, then dashed through the gate, up the stairs, and into the school. I was safe. Yeah, right. Five CGs walking down the hall saw me and their eyes lit up. "Hey, look! It's the mouse!" "Don't you brush your hair, mouse? Or are there bugs in it so you can't?" "Huh, mouse?"

Tears pricked my eyes. The girls came closer, pushing me down the hall. Where were the teachers? Why weren't they in the halls? Then I realized one of the CGs had probably faked a faint or a fever, or pretended to fall down the steps, calling for help from the staff and distracting them. Their plan was well plotted and well executed. I was in trouble. Then, wonder of wonders, the final bell rang. The girls split as the yard staff and students spilled in. It was over. I was safe, right?

Wrong. For weeks after that, the CGs followed me. The participants switched around, but one girl was always there—Eve Thipault, their leader.

My grades slipped. My parents asked me what was wrong, but I couldn't tell them. I had already envisioned what would happen if they called the principal and the girls found out I had told. Life would be a zillion times worse. So I kept quiet.

However, my older sister Sirit had noticed the strange expressions on my face every day when I got home, as I crumpled the nasty notes I'd received. One day in November she pulled me into our shared room, shut the door, and sat me on her bed.

"Elenny, what's wrong?" Her face looked so serious, so caring. I caved. My face buried in her shoulder, I cried out the whole story—the apples, the chasing, the notes, the whole thing. For what felt like hours she sat there, listening. Then, when I was done, she sat me up.

"El," she said, "tell me something that's wrong with Eve's looks."

"What?"

"C'mon," she urged.

I thought hard, imagining my enemy's perfect hair, body, clothes, shoes . . . .

"It's her face!"

"What?" Sirit looked surprised.

"Her face!" I was giggling now. "Her face is shaped like a monkey's!" For a split second, Sirit looked at me like I was crazy. Then she began to howl with laughter. We rocked on the bed, laughing at my enemy's face as I described every detail.

"You know what?" my sister finally said, wiping her eyes, "just look at her face tomorrow. Then everything will be fine."

The next day, feeling almost sick with nervousness, but free from dread, I walked to school. No bullies were out—it was too cold for their lingerie-like clothes. I crept into school and walked toward the east locker bank. As I reached it, the CGs came into view, waiting for me as usual. As they got going, I felt tears welling up. Then I remembered my sister's words of advice. I looked at Eve's face, into her eyes.

I began to giggle. I laughed, guffawed, and even howled. I had to bend over to control myself. "What are you laughing at?" snarled Eve.

"You!" I gasped as I fought for breath. "All of you!" I leaned against the wall, still grinning, but no longer laughing. "All of you think you're so perfect! That you're better than us! You go around trying to find weak, imperfect people, when you just have to look in the mirror!"

I heard a giggle and turned. Two girls and a boy were standing behind me. The whole hallway had been silent, but now everyone began to laugh. I walked up to Eve and offered to shake hands in truce, but she pulled back. "Fine," I said. "Be a bad sport." I walked away.

After that, Eve left the CGs and switched to another schedule. I never saw her except in the halls between fifth and sixth periods. I made three friends—the kids from the hallway—Mike, Sarah, and Anna.

On the last day of school, Eve came up to me and stuck out her hand. "Hey," she said, looking red from embarrassment, "I'm sorry about, you know . . . ."

"Yes, I'm sorry too," I told her. "But it's over now, isn't it?" She nodded. Good. Then I straightened up and marched out of school.

Abby is thirteen and lives in Arlington, Virginia. Abby loves to write because it relaxes her. When she puts her feelings down on paper, she gets so into it she forgets where she is. Writing is a key ingredient to her life, particularly when it's fiction!

GIRLS RULE!

"If you can dream it, you can do it."
—*Walt Disney*

Surprise of a Lifetime
By Farah

"Why did I have to sign up for the Prehistoric Dig-up?" I asked myself as I walked on the cracked, rocky canyon. I struggled along with the sun hitting me in the eyes. Then, suddenly, shade poured on my face like water pouring into a waterfall. I stopped for a second, realizing it was a cave entrance, and ran inside, ready to hog up all the shade. I slumped myself down and kicked a rock, which flew across the cave and hit the other side. Sand began pouring down, revealing a— wait a second, I am getting ahead of myself. Sorry, I have to stop, but I need to so you will enjoy the story!!!

Here is how it began.

"Mommy!" I yelled, with great excitement. "I have to join the one-and-only-filled-with-glory Prehistoric Dig-up!" I tried to imitate a salesman, saying "All you need to do is call in the next five minutes! The number is (555) 123-4567, call right now! That number again is (555) 123-4567." My mom knew there was nothing I wanted more in this world than to go the Prehistoric Dig-up. It would be a dream come true. But she wasn't going to make it easy.

"Farah, there is no such number as (555) 123-4567, and you are not going to be part of the Prehistoric Dig-up Festival until I know more about it."

"Pleeeeease," I said, in a baby voice. Then I toughened up. "I have the real number in my backpack."

"Okay, fine, go get the number. Now move it, before I change my mind."

I gave my mom the number, and she called them up. She spoke softly into the phone. I crept up in order to hear the conversation, but my mom shooed me away by pushing her hand back and forth.

After about five minutes she hung up the phone. Impatiently I blurted out, "What just happened? Am I going? What did they say? Are they going to do it? When are they going to do it?" The questions just slopped out of my mouth like meat slops out of a grinder.

"Slow down honey," my mom said. "Yes, they are going to have the festival, and yes, you are going. They are doing it on Saturday."

I wanted her to repeat it but all I could say was "Ohhhhhhhh!!! Yes, yes, yes, thank you, thank you, thank you."

On Saturday I was jumping with joy, searching through my closet looking for the perfect clothes. I chose an outfit and walked downstairs, buttoning my shirt. My mom said, "You are not wearing that. Go upstairs and go straight to the bathroom." I did, and there on the towel rack was a professional archaeologist's outfit with my name printed on the left-hand side!

I grabbed it, ran downstairs, gave my mom a hug, ran back upstairs, put the outfit on, and ran downstairs again. Mom had made breakfast but I was too excited to eat.

Mom and I got in the car and we were off to the Prehistoric Dig-up Festival. "Are we there yet?" I kept asking my mom. "Are we there yet? Are we there yet?" And every time she would say no, not yet. Then finally I heard the magic words, "Yes we are!!!" My head was spinning, and I thought, yeah we are finally here, oh my gosh what do I do, where do I go first, I am so excited!

My mom left and I stood alone in the hot, sizzling sun. I put my hand over my eyes and noticed my friend Hannah standing there, too, all pumped up. I ran over and asked if I could be her Prehistoric Dig-up partner. She agreed and we were off.

We walked down a steep hill, found some fossils, and picked them up and put them in our bucket. Hannah suggested we stop and dig to see what we could find. We did a lot of digging, searching for something interesting. Dirt was all over my face and body and it was hot. Hannah patted me on my shoulder and it hurt so bad that I knew I was sunburned. From the corner of my eye I saw a scorpion climbing up my shoe. I jumped and started running. So many scary, horrible things were happening to me. I started walking back up the cracked, rocky canyon. Why had I signed up for this in the first place?

I struggled along with the sun hitting me in the eyes. Then, suddenly, shade poured on my face like water pouring into a waterfall. I stopped for a second, realizing it was a cave entrance, and ran inside, ready to hog up all the shade. I slumped myself down and kicked a rock, which flew across the cave and hit the other side. Sand began pouring down, revealing a little niche. It was just big enough for one person to fit in.

Hannah had come into the cave as well. I offered to let her to go into the niche first, and she did.

"FARAH!" she yelled, then came back out. I rushed in to see for myself.

"It's a . . . it's a . . . it's a baby deer!" she shouted. "It is a skeleton of what looks like a baby deer. Quick, you have to go and get the counselor!"

"Hannah, you stay here," I said. "I will get her."

Ten minutes later . . .

The dig leader looked at our find. "Wow, it looks like the skeletal remains of a baby deer," she said. "We have to get the people from the museum here right away. No one touch a thing. You girls are going to be heroes!"

One month later, a newspaper article read:

The skeletal remains of a baby deer have been found in a local cave. The skeleton is thought to be about 150 years old. It was found by Hannah and Farah. If you would like to see these amazing remains, come to the Seattle Art Museum, where they are on display. Hannah and Farah discovered the remains while on a Prehistoric Dig. They came across a cave and while exploring it found the skeleton. A great find, indeed. Hannah and Farah were given the title "Kid Archaeologists of the Year" and are giving tours of the bones at the museum.

What a wonderful time I had, and what an experience. I don't think anything could top it, but who knows? Next summer I am planning to go the Sahara Desert.

Farah is ten years old and lives in Seattle, Washington. She likes writing because it is pure fun, and she loves entertaining people with her creations.

Cassidy Jenkens: Future Superstar
By Erin

"Well, Cassidy, come up and share your essay with us," Mrs. Lindstrom said. Cassidy brushed her skirt and grabbed her hot pink piece of paper. She stepped up to the front of the class.

"'What I Want to Be in Fifteen Years,' by me, Cassidy Jenkens," she began. "In fifteen years, I plan on being a fabulous superstar. I will be famous for singing and acting and I will star in sixty-seven movies and release twenty-three albums. All of my movies will be smashes at the box office, and my albums will be quadruple platinum. I will live in a mansion. My mansion will be hot pink and have special gates and things at the front. I will have nine butlers and nine maids to fulfill my every want and need. I will also have a pool and a Jacuzzi . . . ."

Cassidy was about to explain about the lavish waterfall flowing into her pool when she realized her whole English class was laughing at her. She felt herself turn red. Even Mrs. Lindstrom was laughing!

"Miss Jenkens, how about this? You write a *realistic* essay and turn it in tomorrow," the teacher said. Cassidy was humiliated as she sulked to her desk and slumped in her seat.

After school, Cassidy ran off of the bus and into her room. She flopped onto her bed. She was still so embarrassed, and she really felt tired. She started to drift off . . . .

Cassidy opened her eyes and looked around. She was on a pool lounge chair. She looked down and saw that she was wearing the dream diamond swimsuit from her essay. And there was a pool! And a Jacuzzi, and a huge hot pink mansion! Cassidy got up and walked around.

"Pink lemonade, Miss Jenkens?"

Cassidy turned to see a butler and answered, "Yes, please!" He handed her the lemonade as she walked into her mansion. Unbelievable! The place was *dripping* with diamonds and hot pink objects. And there were movie posters from Cassidy's hit films and platinum CDs mounted on the wall. She was about to open a door that read "Cassidy's Bedroom" but . . . .

"Cassidy! Cassidy! Dinnertime!" Cassidy blinked. She was in her own room again. She checked the time. 6:45! She'd been sleeping for hours. She started to go downstairs when she noticed something. There, on her nightstand, was something that proved her dreams would come true.

It was a cup of perfect pink lemonade.

Erin is thirteen and lives in Lee's Summit, Missouri. She loves writing about girls and their lives, and she really likes writing about famous girls because she wants to be famous someday!